THE FARMER
FAMILY ALBUM

THE FARMER
FAMILY ALBUM

CHESTER G. THOMPSON

THE FARMER FAMILY ALBUM

iUniverse books may be ordered through booksellers or by contacting:

iUniverse
1663 Liberty Drive
Bloomington, IN 47403
www.iuniverse.com
1-800-Authors (1-800-288-4677)

Because of the dynamic nature of the Internet, any web addresses or links contained in this book may have changed since publication and may no longer be valid. The views expressed in this work are solely those of the author and do not necessarily reflect the views of the publisher, and the publisher hereby disclaims any responsibility for them.

Any people depicted in stock imagery provided by Thinkstock are models, and such images are being used for illustrative purposes only.
Certain stock imagery © Thinkstock.

ISBN: 978-1-4917-9326-8 (sc)
ISBN: 978-1-4917-9344-2 (e)

Library of Congress Control Number: 2016905115

Print information available on the last page.

iUniverse rev. date: 04/28/2016

THIS BOOK IS DEDICATED
IN MEMORY OF

Donna Gay Thompson
Born March 18th, 1945 at Phoenix, Arizona
Entered Into Rest On
September 4th, 2006 at Peoria, Arizona
My Co-Author

INTRODUCTION

The old oak tree house aired on KLKY radio in 1988. However some changes were made. Our house really did have oak floors and we still have the old grandfather clock.

How the donkey Dan show happened was on the air in 1987. It is basically the true story of how the show came about.

The donkey that believed God aired in 1990. It was kept pretty much in its original form.

The idea came from the donkey jaw bone found in the story, taken from the Old Testament about Samson.

The story of the cabbage inn aired in 1988–89 and was done by me on the radio after Donna took ill. I did several science broadcast for the children as well as interested adults. This was one of the first in a series of scientific programs I did.

Bonkers was actually two broadcast. Bonkers first snow aired in 1990. On that show we needed a very short story because we needed the room for music and another short story which I also added to the end of this book it was called: We dig dirt.

It's the night before Christmas was written for a broadcast by me. I believe for a December 1989 show. The idea was taken from the original poem penned in

1803 by Henry Livingston and published for the first time by New York's Troy Sentinel on December 23, 1823.

The amazing honey bee aired in 1989 a few broadcast after the cabbage inn. I have always liked and respected the honey bee. This story remains very much like its original except a little more text was added.

The story of big red was on one of our shows in late 1990. I wrote it in honor of a very friendly, big, two toned red and protective hero rooster. Red allowed us to pick him up and hold him anytime we desired. He however was killed protecting his hens from a pair of stray dogs on a very wet stormy night. I discovered the scene the next morning. His favorite hen was found behind red in her nest box alive.

CONTENTS

CHAPTER ONE

THE OLD OAK TREE HOUSE

Once upon a very long time ago, in a very nice forest there lived a very special family. They were called the farmer family.

Sammy was the daddy skunk and Daphne was the momma skunk of the family. Bonkers was the family's orange tabby cat. Tremor was the wee skate boarding mouse that lived in a tiny mouse hole behind the old grandfather clock. The older son was a teenage porcupine named Erasmus. The younger son was a nine year old roadrunner named Ewald. The family lived in a trailer house with Bonkers their cat on a tiny farm.

Then one bad day, their house caught fire and burned to the ground. But thank God even old Bonkers the cat got out okay. They began to search the forest for a new place to live. Just a few miles away they found a meadow. In the center of this meadow stood a large old oak tree that would be a good home.

It was nice on the outside with five windows cut out of knots in the trunk. They went inside to look around. It hadn't been lived in for some time but it was nice.

In the living room they found a small hole in the baseboard. Sammy and Erasmus would place the grandfather clock that Daphne bought in front of it.

After the inside of the house was cleaned and their new furniture was in place, Sammy and the boys went to work outside. They built a chicken house, dug a garden area, built a goat pen with a shelter and fenced off a pasture for their new friend donkey Dan. While this was being done Daphne was in the kitchen getting dinner ready.

Meanwhile Bonkers the orange stripped cat was sound asleep in the window of the oak tree house. Cats like to nap in the warmth of the sun coming through a window. Momma skunk rang the dinner bell and soon the family was sitting around their new oak table. Daphne skunk led the prayer and added a thank you for the new house at the end. After all their hard labor they really did eat and momma skunk was glad she cooked so much food. They all were so tired that momma skunk left the dishes by the sink to be washed in the morning. They went right to bed and all was quiet in the old oak tree house.

Or was it? Sammy and Daphne were asleep; Erasmus and Ewald were also asleep. Bonkers was now sleeping on his rug in front of the fireplace. The only noise seemed to be the steady tick tock of the grandfather clock.

Wait, did you hear that soft little sound coming from behind the clock? I thought you might hear it and so did someone else.

I'll bet you can guess who that was. Bonkers was sure he heard a strange noise so his eyes popped open; he sat up and looked around the dark room. Cats have good eyes that can see in the dark and their ears can hear the softest little sound. It was quiet for several minutes, so Bonkers lay back down and was soon fast asleep once again.

After about forever, the noise started up once again but even more softly than before. This time even the cat who was very asleep didn't hear the soft sounds. Suddenly from across the room a tiny little creature riding a tiny skate board went right past Bonkers.

He was heading under the table toward a nice big piece of cheese that someone dropped on the floor during dinner.

Bonkers slept right through the whole thing until the wee mouse turned and headed back across the room toward the grandfather clock. Tremor was so happy about the cheese that he accidentally ran his skate board right up the cat's tail, over his head and down his nose. It all happened so fast that the cat didn't even have time to know what had happened. Bonkers let out the loudest and most scary screech that anyone has ever heard. Sammy jumped so high he fell out of bed onto the floor.

Momma skunk jumped to her feet as Ewald and Erasmus ran into the living room. When Sammy finally got up and shook himself, he also headed for the living room to see what was going on. He arrived just in time to see Bonkers hanging from the curtains wide eyed and shaking from head to tail.

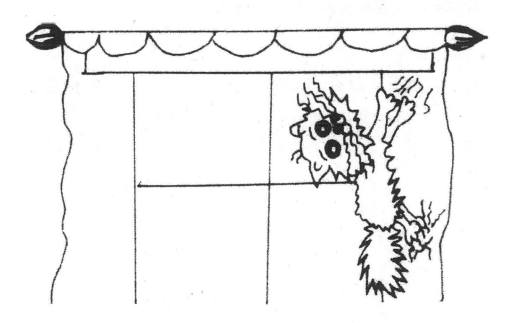

Behind the clock in his little mouse hole Tremor was shaking all over with his whiskers twitching very fast. "A cat, a very big cat, I skate boarded up the back of a cat," squeaked little Tremor.

It was a long time before Tremor could stop shaking, crawl out from under his bed and eat his cheese.

After he had finished his meal, Tremor crawled off to bed. Bonkers never did sleep the rest of the night because with every noise his eyes would pop open.

Because of being so very tired from all of the work the boys slipped into sleep as soon as their heads hit the pillows. Daphne also tired went back to sleep real quick.

Sammy on the other hand laid awake for a long while trying to figure out what in world happened. Then finally with a sigh he fell asleep.

All was really quiet in the old oak tree house.

CHAPTER TWO

HOW THE DONKEY DAN SHOW HAPPENED

"Sammy! You'll never guess what happened today", said momma skunk. It seems that Daphne was walking and praying about nothing special, when all of a sudden, she knew that God wanted to tell her something. "He seemed to speak almost audibly", said momma skunk. "What did He tell you," asked Sammy? " 'Go put this on the radio,' He told me. I answered, 'You have got to be kidding me!' " "Well maybe you had better go into Prescott to one of the radio stations", said Sammy. Daphne left for Prescott to find a radio station that would allow her some time to put what God told her to say on the radio. The first station she went to told her that she could have sixty seconds if she paid the fee they charged advertisers. When she got back Sammy asked her what happened. "You can believe this because it is true! What God gave me is already on the radio in one day. And it will be broadcasted all over Yavapai county in ten minutes", stated Daphne! Momma skunk turned on the radio and changed it to the correct station. It May have been short but it sounded good to Sammy.

After the radio was turned off, Daphne continued telling Sammy what led up to her being put on the radio. She said the man told her she had to sound professional or he wouldn't put it on and he didn't want any religious stuff. But the Lord worked out everything so well that the man placed it on the radio anyway. "Maybe the Lord is telling you that you'd be good on the radio", said Sammy. "No! I don't think so because I'd sound dumb on the radio", replied Momma skunk. Sammy didn't see anything wrong with her voice and he told her so. "It would be fun but I would sound like a little girl", whined Daphne. But she did what he told her and called the station. When she hung up the phone, she told Sammy what the man had said. "The grumpy old guy said he didn't want any more religious stuff on his station. He did say that he would charge forty- seven dollars, for fifteen minutes and he would only let us have 5:00 a.m."

They both laughed and Sammy went out to feed the animals. In a few minutes he came back into the house and stood next to Daphne's chair and said, "Why don't you call our local Prescott Valley station"? "Are you serious Sammy? Maybe God only wanted me to do that broadcast and that's all," said Daphne. After a few minutes she told him that she would give it another try and so she called K.L.K.Y. radio of Prescott Valley.

When she hung up, she just sat there staring off into space. "What did they say", asked Sammy? Momma skunk's face lit up and she began to tell was said on the phone. "The station manager was real nice and he said we could have fifteen minutes and seven free commercials for our program for just $30.00 anytime on Sunday mornings. But he wants us to come up with a theme song for our program", said Daphne. "But we have almost no music since the fire that burned up everything that we owned," continued Momma skunk. Erasmus walked into the room at that very moment and said he just copied a song off the radio. He said it was a cute song and he wanted them to hear it. After listening to the song they both agreed it would be the perfect theme song because it was such a cute song about Jesus riding on a donkey.

At church that night, two more prayers were answered and even more the next day. Pastor Teddy Bear's sermon was the exact passage in the Bible that the theme song was taken from. The mention of the donkey seemed to jump from the page for daddy skunk. And so it was decided that the name of the show would be "The Donkey Dan Show". The station manager came up with the slogan "For Kids From 2 to 92." They had people of all ages and walks of life tuning into "The Donkey Dan Show: on K.L.K.Y. every Sunday morning while they were getting ready to go to church. The real Donkey Dan came to live with the family soon after their first show.

Then all was quiet in the old oak tree house.

CHAPTER THREE

THE DONKEY THAT BELIEVED GOD

Sammy was sitting in his favorite chair eating an apple. "Dad could you tell us a story?" asked Ewald. "Yes could you", added Randy raccoon. "Actually I was just thinking about a story. But first let me finish my apple", said Sammy. Erasmus and Eddie beaver were sitting at the table playing a game. Daphne was in the kitchen putting up the lunch dishes.

Tremor was nibbling on an apple core that he'd found outside. Tremor was always ready for one of Sammy's stories.

When he finished his apple, Sammy began the story. Once many years ago in a country far from here called Israel there was a young white donkey. This little donkey believed that God spoke to him. The donkey just knew that God told him, "You will be used mightily".

He was so excited that he told his friends the sheep and goats. Some of the goats believed what he told them. However none of the sheep could believe a donkey could be used by God. After all they reasoned, sheep are used in the temple and donkeys aren't, they are used to do hard work. "How mean", exclaimed Ewald and Randy at the same time! By this time Erasmus and Eddie beaver gave up playing their game and came in to sit on the couch. "I guess the story is more interesting", teased Ewald. Daphne who also wanted to hear the story came in and sat in her chair. Sammy just continued on with the story. The sheep believed that they were of more value to God then a mere donkey. After all some sheep were taken into the temple grounds every year and were allowed to stay. This kind of thinking is what made the sheep so prideful.

Soon the weeks became months and the months turned into years. All of this time, the sheep were saying things like I thought you said God was going to use you. One would always say something like God would never use a donkey for anything and especially not for something important. "That shows just how really dumb the sheep were," said Randy. "That's right", God used donkeys several times in the bible", exclaimed Ewald! The now teenage donkey simply repeated what God had told him. "I'll bet he's the donkey that carried Mary to Bethlehem", said Ewald. "I'm afraid not", said daddy skunk. "Was he the one that carried Jesus into Jerusalem", asked Randy? "Not that donkey either", replied Sammy. "Was he Balaam's donkey", asked Eddie? But Sammy just shook his head no. Then he laughed and continued his story. The years passed by and most of his friends were tired talking about how God would use the donkey. Some of the sheep would still ask, "Why hasn't God used you yet"? The donkey would only say, "I believe Him". This making fun of the donkey seemed to be a daily thing among the younger sheep. But as the years passed the now old donkey would only say, "I don't know why God hasn't used me yet but He said He would so He will".

Another few years went by and the once young and strong donkey was now very old, slow, and weak. "You mean like grandfather", asked Ewald? "Yes like grandpa", answered Daddy Skunk. Then one day he began to climb a hill and with a lot of effort he made it to the top. He was very tired, so he found a soft spot in the grass and lay down to rest. But the little donkey never got back up because he died. "Goodness", exclaimed Eddie beaver! "You're kidding right dad", said Erasmus. "Good grief", exclaimed Ewald and Randy at the same time! "What a very sad ending", remarked Daphne. "Sad ending, Who said, it was the end of the story", asked daddy skunk? As Sammy continued he said, "It took three days before the sheep and goats noticed the donkey was missing". The goats sent out a search party that looked all over the pasture. The sheep just couldn't be bothered after all they weren't their brother's keeper. Finally the eldest goat looked on top of the hill and there was the donkey. The old goat called out and all of the goats and sheep came to the top of the hill. "Well at least the goats missed him", squeaked Tremor from behind the clock.

Most of the sheep said they knew that the donkey didn't hear from God. Besides why would God bother to use a donkey when there are plenty of sheep? The oldest ram said, "God can't use a dead donkey that's for sure". Then the sheep left the hill. The oldest he goat watched them leave and said, "I wonder". then he looked down at the donkey and said, "At least he's happy now"!

It was about a year later, when an Israelite was on that same hill battling the enemies of Israel. These were called the Philistines and were enemies of God. The Israelites name was Samson. He looked around for anything that could be used as a weapon. "So that was the donkey", exclaimed Erasmus! "Yep, that's the one", said Sammy. When Samson was looking down, he saw the donkey's jaw-bone. He picked it up and killed all of the enemy soldiers. So God can even use a dead donkey", said momma. "God did use the little donkey mightily just like he promised he would. His jaw bone saved all of Israel that day on the hill", said Sammy. "Wow, what a great story", said Ewald. Tremor who was still sitting on his thimble behind the clock had tears in his eyes. Sammy went out to feed the animals. The family didn't know it but donkey Dan, who had very good ears, also heard the story. So when Sammy put the hay in the feed trough, the donkey licked Sammy's face and smiled as best as a donkey could.

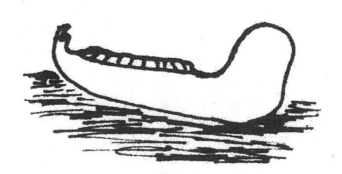

Then all was quiet in the old oak tree house.

CHAPTER FOUR

THE CABBAGE INN

Behind the grandfather clock Tremor mouse was sitting on his thimble chair at the entrance of his little mouse house. He did this every evening when Sammy sat in his chair by the fireplace. Tremor found that the rest of the family would often come into the living room and somehow they would get Sammy to tell a story. Tonight was no exception. Momma skunk was in her chair reading and Ewald was on the couch just looking at the fire. Erasmus who had been in his room doing homework came in with a frown and very upset. Momma skunk asked why he was so upset. He told her that his teacher Mr. Badger was a real old grump. Then he plopped down next to Ewald on the couch. Daphne reminded her son that it wasn't nice to call someone a name even in fun. Sammy asked what Mr. Badger did this time? He said he would flunk me in biology if I wrote on my test that God created everything, instead of saying everything evolved. "What! That crazy old grump", said momma skunk. Sammy just rolled his eyes and sighed.

"That reminds me of a true story which I call the cabbage inn", said daddy skunk. "The cabbage what", exclaimed Ewald the little road runner! "The cabbage inn, It's like a cabbage motel", answered Erasmus the teenage porcupine. Meanwhile

Tremor mouse was all ears because he loved stories and this one was a true story. Even old Bonkers the cat's ears perked up as he lay by the warm fireplace. To begin with Sammy explained that it wasn't a place but more of a thing. Out in the swamp very early in the spring a funny purple plant opens her house for vacationing bees and a few other insects.

Even meals are served inside the plant, which is toasty and warm. It is one of God's most unusual flowering plants. "I'll bet it eats the bees like the venus fly trap right dad" asked Ewald? "Who is telling this story me or you", asked Sammy? "Sorry dad", said Ewald. Sammy just smiled and told him that it didn't eat its guest. This plant is called the skunk cabbage and it loves the rich soil of the swamp-lands. The plants root goes at least a foot deep into the earth. This anchors it firmly in the wet soil. In summer, it has broad leaves nearly two feet tall and a soft head of bright green cabbage in the center.

"We should go find some to eat", Interrupted Erasmus. "Look boys stop interrupting your father or we may never get to eat our dinner", laughed momma skunk. "This isn't a cabbage that you would enjoy eating", said Sammy. The skunk cabbage lives in the swamp and if a whitetail deer were to find one and take a nibble it gives off a strong skunk like odor that stops it from taking a second bite. Because of that smell animals and plant eating insects leave it alone. This is God's way of keeping it from harm because he has an important job for the cabbage.

The root of the cabbage produces a plant evert spring and the root can live longer than an oak tree. Every spring while the snow is still on the ground the root sends out a hood shaped leaf called a spathe. This leaf is purple and yellow and shaped like the hood of a gnome.

It's pointed at the top and slightly bent over with an opening that you might expect to see a gnomes face sticking out of. Inside this hood is a ball with several yellow flowers on a stem. If bee flies anywhere near the plant, it gives off an ultraviolet light that reflects in the bee's eyes and attracts it to the flowers. The bee gets the nectar and the pollen is sent by bee to another skunk cabbage. This in turn causes seeds to form and when they mature they fall to the damp soil and produce other new plant growing roots. This isn't unusual for plants to do. The real thing that makes the skunk cabbage one of god's special creations is it's furnace. Scientist have taken the temperature inside of the hood and found that it is a constant 72 degrees even if it's 18degrees outside. "How does It do it", asked Ewald? "Glad you asked", said daddy skunk. It actually burns oxygen as a fuel at a very fast rate with the specially designed cells it has. The cells in the flower stem actually have thermostats that keep the temperature 72 inside the hood. The cabbage inn is just one piece of evidence that there is a designer of some kind. "I think that as smart as he is Mr. Badger is wrong but if I were you I would answer his test questions by what your book says. That way you'll get a good grade even if you believe the book is wrong", said Sammy. "I think I will give Mr. Badger a piece of my mind", exclaimed momma skunk! "I don't think you should do that because you need all the pieces you have", said daddy skunk. Momma skunk laughed and so did the boys but only after she did first.

Late the next afternoon, Erasmus burst through the door and jumped for joy as he told the whole family that he had passed his test. The whole family was happy to hear the good news. Even Tremor jumped to his feet and cheered so loud that Bonkers heard him and walked over to the grandfather clock sniffing the air. Tremor ducked under his little bed. Finally the cat gave up and went back to the fireplace to lie down. About an hour later the family was eating and so was Tremor.

And all was quiet in the old oak tree house.

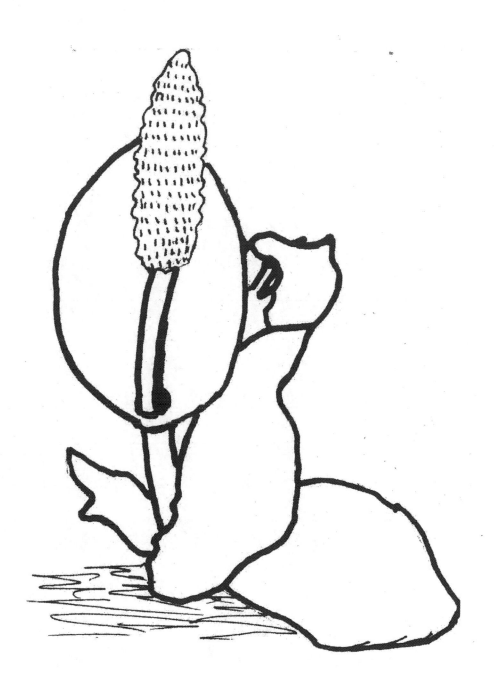

CHAPTER FIVE

BONKERS FIRST SNOW

One winter evening, when everyone had returned home from visiting with Sammy's brother and his family, Sammy went out to feed the animals. Ewald who was looking out the window at the time, called Erasmus over to see the first snow of the year. The snow had been falling fast and built up to about one foot on the ground.

All of a sudden Erasmus said, "Look Ewald, bonkers slipped out the door behind dad".

Most cats love to sneak out when their owners go out the door. Bonkers who had never seen snow before took one step off the porch. Erasmus had to run fast to open the door for the cat. Ewald, who was laughing exclaimed, "You won't believe me when I tell you what I just saw"!

"Our silly old Bonkers just jumped a foot into the air, turned while in mid-air and landed on the porch running for the door", said Ewald!

"I barely got the door open before Bonkers got there. Then guess what happened", said Erasmus. "What did", asked momma skunk? It seems the cat who had wet feet slid across the floor and into the wall before going under the table. Tremor was listening when the boys told Sammy what Bonkers had done. At the end of the tale Tremor began to laugh so hard that he fell off his thimble and rolled on the floor. "That silly old cat", laughed Tremor. "I wonder why I'm so scared of such a silly old cat", remarked Tremor as he got up from the floor.

Everyone got ready to go to bed. Even Bonkers finally came out from under the table and went to his spot by the fireplace. "I wish I could be braver", squeaked the little mouse. Then he climbed into his bed for the night. Everyone was soon fast asleep.

All was quiet in the old oak tree house.

CHAPTER SIX

DO YOU WISH??

Do you wish you'd live in Bethlehem,

that first glad Christmas Night?

Do you wish you'd seen the glorious star,

with it's bright and shining light?

Do you wish you'd been a witness,

to the great things happening then?

Do you wish the star of Christmas,

would appear to you again?

Then I wonder would you see it?

Do you look for things afar?

Do you look beyond the everyday,

for a bright and shinning star?

Or are you burdened with the giving

and the duties you obey

Till you loose the Christ like spirit

of the first true Christmas day.

Would you go to a lowly stable,
as the shepherds did that Night?
Or does the glitter of this world
blind you to the Christ child's light?

For the church is the stable of long ago
and the altar, His manger bed.
Do you love Him enough today my friend
to come and by him be led?

Dear Lord, help us to go to church
to give our lives to thee.
Take us to your manger bed,
And from this world set free.

CHAPTER SEVEN

THE AMAZING HONEY BEE

Sammy was sitting by the fireplace in his favorite chair and Bonkers the orange tabby cat was asleep as usual on the hearth. The family had just finished eating dinner and Daphne was doing the dishes and cleaning the table. Ewald and Erasmus were on the couch. Tremor was on his thimble behind the grandfather clock waiting for Sammy to tell a story which most always happened after dinner. Tremor noticed that lately many of the stories had science in them. The little mouse loved to learn about nature so he loved the stories about God's creation. Suddenly Ewald broke the silence by saying, "My friend Randy raccoon was stung by a bee today while we were playing in the pasture". "Did you know that some small animals and even people can die from even one bee sting", added Erasmus into the conversation. "My brother is one of those people", exclaimed momma skunk who really didn't like bees! "How is that even possible when bees are so small", asked Ewald? "Well, some people are allergic to the venom that the bee injects with its stinger. But did you know a honey bee can only sting once because the stinger tares out and the bee dies", said daddy skunk.

"No other creature God created has served the needs of people like that tiny insect we call the honey bee", said Sammy as he began to tell the story of the honey bee. For centuries people have been bee keepers. They harvest the sweet honey that the bees produce and count on the bees to pollinate many crops. Actually the little ladies pollinate about 1/3 of all the food crops we eat, in fact without the bee the world would have less food and beauty in it. "That means many animals would starve to death", said Erasmus the teenage porcupine. "Yes and many plants would become extinct", said Sammy. Honey bees can fly about 15 miles per hour.

A colony of bees can have as many as 60,000 bees in it. "Wow, that is a lot of bees!" exclaimed Ewald. "Ouch that is a lot of stings", stated Erasmus. The workers are all females and are almost all we ever see. Honey bees are social insects and the bees in the hive are divided into three groups. The largest group in number is the workers which are all females that are not developed to lay eggs. They do all the work in and outside of the hive. Some of their jobs are scouting for food sources, guarding the hive, building the hive, being the undertaker, cleaning the hive, circulating the air in the hive and to groom and feed the queen as well as many other jobs. "I hope they get paid good", laughed Ewald. Sammy just laughed and continued on. "The next group in he hive is the smallest in number. Can you guess what that group is", asked Sammy? "Sure it's the queen", answered momma skunk. The queen lives three to four years and has one job and that is to lay eggs. She lays up to 1,500 eggs in a day and can lay about a million in her lifetime. "That is a lot of eggs no wonder she lives such a short time," Erasmus said.

She can produce her own body weight in eggs in just one day. The hive normally has just one queen and if she dies, the workers will create a new queen by feeding one of their sister workers a diet of "Royal Jelly". This diet enables that worker to become a queen.

Queens also regulates the hives activities by giving off chemicals that guide the behavior of the bees. The last group in the colony is the males which are called drones. There can be several hundred drones in a hive in the spring and summer months. In the winter the colony goes into survival mode and since the drones are no longer needed they are chased out into the cold to die. "How awful", exclaimed Ewald! During the winter the colony lives on the honey they stored.

But by spring the hive is swarming with the next generation of honey bees. When the colony gets too big the workers feed Royal Jelly to one or more larva in order to make extra queens. The workers will keep the queens away from each other because the queens will fight to the death. Then when the time is right the colony will divide and one or more swarms will leave to start new colonies.

"Did you know that bees talk to each other by using sign language", asked Sammy? "How on earth do they do that when they don't have hands", asked Erasmus? "Well let me continue and you will find out", said daddy skunk. Honey bees use a most complex symbolic language. In fact it is the most complex symbolic language of any of God's creatures on earth, except for members of the primate family. In 1973 a professor and researcher won the Nobel prize for interpreting the language of the honey bees. The bees use movement and odor cues to share information with the rest of the colony. "What kind of movements", asked Ewald? "They do a sort of dance that people call the waggle dance", answered Sammy. It is a series of movements a scout will use to teach the rest of the workers the location of a food source. "That sounds like a very hard way to give others directions", said Ewald.

"Not really, when you think about someone hunting with other hunters who might just point to the prey and place their hand over their mouth to tell the others to be quiet", said Sammy. "I have seen soldiers in movies hold up a hand and close their fingers to signal others to stop moving", added Erasmus. When the scout returns to the hive she dances on the honey comb first by shaking her back end and using her wings to make a buzzing sound. The distance and speed of the dance tells the rest of the colony the distance to the food source, relative to the sun. This dance was first observed and noted by Aristotle about 300 B.C.

The workers maintain a constant 93 degrees in the hive summer and winter. As it gets colder outside the bees form a tight group in the hive around the queen to keep warm. Then in the summer they will fan the air within the hive to keep the queen and brood from getting to hot. Honey bee workers make their bees wax from special glands. The youngest workers take on this job of making the bees wax used to build the combs.

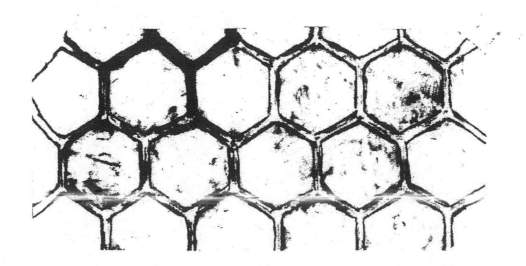

They have eight pairs of glands on their underside that put out wax droplets. These harden into flakes as soon as they hit the air. So the workers have to soften them in their mouths before building the combs. These honey and brood combs are both built in a hexagon shape so that they take up less room and use less wax. How they build a perfect hexagon only God knows. "Honey bees are sure amazing insects", whispered Tremor the mouse because he saw Bonkers the orange tabby sniffing around the grandfather clock. "They should really put a bell on that cat", thought Tremor. A hard working bee may visit 2,000 flowers in a day. She will visit 50 or more in one trip and make as many trips as she can in a day. "This puts real wear on her tiny body and she may only live just three weeks", said Sammy. "I think I will look at the bee very differently from now on", exclaimed momma skunk! "What a short little life for such an amazing creature", said Erasmus. "I think God should give them at least a year of life", chimed in Ewald. "God sure created some interesting and complex creatures when He created the little honey bees", squeaked Tremor as he slid into bed.

Then all was quiet in the old oak tree house.

CHAPTER EIGHT

BIG RED

"Dad how did big Red come to live with us", asked Ewald? "Yeah dad you never told us his story", said Erasmus. "That's right you boys were away at camp when we brought Red home", said daddy skunk. So Sammy began the story of big Red the rooster. Sammy had several young hens in his chicken coop but he wanted a nice red rooster. He was watching the news paper ads for anyone giving away or selling poultry. Then one day he saw an ad that was for a free rooster. Sammy called the phone number in the ad right away and was told that it was a big Red rooster. The minute he saw the rooster he liked it. The owners said he liked being held and he was a very friendly half Rhode Island Red and half Ameraucana rooster. When they got home Daphne had Sammy take a picture of her holding big Red. Red really liked being the only rooster in the hen house. He seemed to like all of the hens, but he did have a favorite one and spent most of his time near her.

The big red rooster would crow at sun up then wait to be fed and turned loose to go into the pasture with his family. "He is a happy rooster in his new home", said Sammy. "Yes he is, said Daphne, and we are glad to have him also", she continued.

Donkey Dan seemed to enjoy Red's company in the pasture, and Tremor loved to wake up to his crowing at the break of dawn. Bonkers the cat stayed away from the chickens ever since he tried to pounce on one of the hens. Red ran at the cat pecking his rump and spurring him until Bonkers ran off to the house. The goats enjoyed having the rooster strutting thru the yard and from time to time they allowed him to sit on their backs.

One spring morning Sammy heard what he thought was some baby chicks peeping in the hen house. When he entered to check it out sure enough seven little red chicks were playing what appeared to be rugby with a small piece of paper. Sammy went to the house to tell the rest of the family to come out and see the funny sight. When everyone went back in the house Sammy fed the flock and opened the coop door so they could go into the pasture. The chicks followed their mother out staying close behind her. That's when Sammy found out that big

Reds favorite hen was the mother hen. Sammy sat on a tree stump and watched his flock for about an hour. Sometimes daddy skunk would sit in the porch swing and watch them scratching for seeds or chasing grass hoppers in the back yard.

Today after going back into the house he happened to look out of the window just in time to see the red tailed hawk swoop down toward Rose and her chicks. Rose gave out a warning cry and the chicks darted under her as she lay as flat as she could on the ground. The hawk landed on top of her and was about to rip her apart when from seemingly out of nowhere big Red attacked the hawk. He jumped on the surprised bird of prey with his spurs digging in and his beak pecking it's head. The hawk being no match for the rooster's fury managed to wiggle free and take to the air never to be seen again. Rose was shaken and missing a few feathers but otherwise not hurt. Her brood was standing next to her safe thanks to her quick actions and their fearless protective father.

That night after dinner and when the dishes were done Sammy told the story of big Red and the hawk. Ewald was wide eyed as he said, "Good going big Red". "He sure is one brave rooster that's for sure", said Erasmus. "Sammy, are you sure Rose and her chicks are okay?" asked momma skunk? Meanwhile Tremor jumped off his thimble and yelled, "Good going big Red it's about time someone kicked that hawks tail feathers"! As he so often did he squeaked too loud before thinking and he slapped his paws over his mouth. Then he listened to see if Bonkers was stirring from his cat nap. When the mouse heard no sound from the cat he whispered, "Maybe I should be brave and kick old Bonkers tail". Then after a second thought he said, "Not a good idea".

And all was quiet in the old oak tree house.

Printed in the United States
By Bookmasters